THE GHOST OF SHADY LANE

DOTTI ENDERLE

Llewellyn Publications
Woodbury, Minnesota

FIRST EDITION
Second printing, 2005

Book design and editing by Kimberly Nightingale
Cover design by Kevin R. Brown
Cover illustration and interior illustrations © 2005 by Matthew Archambault

Library of Congress Cataloging-in-Publication Data
Enderle, Dotti, 1954–
The ghost of Shady Lane / Dotti Enderle.—1st Llewellyn Edition
p. cm. [Fortune Tellers Club, the ghost of Shady Lane]
Summary: Creepy, run down, and possibly haunted, "The Boogerman House" becomes the object of Anne's fascination as she researches this historic landmark for a school assignment.
ISBN-10: 0-7387-0590-X (pbk.)
[1. Psychic Ability/Parapsychology/Supernatural/Ghosts/ Clubs—Juvenile fiction 2. Psychic ability/Supernatural/Ghosts/ Clubs—Fiction] I. Title
2005299535

ISBN-13: 978-0-7387-0590-3

Llewellyn Publications
A Division of Llewellyn Worldwide, Ltd.
2143 Wooddale Drive, Dept. 0-7387-0590-X
Woodbury, MN 55125-2989, U.S.A.
www.llewellyn.com

Printed in the United States of America

Fortune Tellers Club

The Ghost of Shady Lane

Other Books by Dotti Enderle

The Lost Girl
Playing with Fire
The Magic Shades
Secrets of Lost Arrow
Hand of Fate
Mirror, Mirror . . .
The Burning Pendulum

Contents

CHAPTER 1

Boogerman's House

"Boogerman's house! Why didn't I think of that?" Juniper said, twirling her empty soda bottle on the floor.

Anne beamed. "Hey, do I know how to pick a subject for social studies, or what? I've always wondered why people think that house is haunted. Now's my chance to investigate. So what landmark did *you* pick?"

"The Lincoln Memorial."

Gena stopped Juniper's bottle in midspin. "I picked Mount Rushmore, a.k.a. 'Our Four Fathers.' She held up four fingers to demonstrate.

"They're not 'Our Four Fathers,' dummy. Where'd you hear that?" Juniper asked.

"From a kid I babysat last year."

Anne laughed and shifted, pulling her knees up into a hug. "Are you sure he wasn't talking about our *forefathers?* As in f-o-r-e? You know, meaning 'before'?"

"Maybe," Gena said. "But don't you think it's more than a coincidence that there are FOUR of them?"

"Oh, jeez," Juniper said, shaking her head.

Gena shrugged. "Oh well, guess I won't be looking that kid up for more info after all."

"Smart idea," Anne said.

Juniper went back to twirling the bottle. "So how are you going to research Boogerman's house? Where are you going to look?"

"There's got to be records somewhere. I mean, where did that historical marker come from anyway?"

"Ah-hum . . . and what about *her?*" Gena asked.

Anne knew exactly who Gena meant. "She'll definitely be part of the report."

Juniper stopped the bottle herself this time. "Who?"

"The Gray Lady!" Anne and Gena blurted at the same time.

Juniper slapped her forehead. "Duh! How could I forget *her?*"

"Do you think it's true?" Anne asked. "That she hanged herself in the attic?"

Juniper nodded. "It's true, but I'm not so sure about the piano music."

"Yeah, what's up with that?" Gena said. "A bunch of kids at school have said they've heard the ghost music when they've gone by, but I've been by that house eight zillion times, and I haven't even heard 'Chopsticks.'"

Anne smirked. "Since when can you believe most of the junk you hear at school? I'm not saying her ghost *isn't* playing the piano in there somewhere. I just don't think too many people have heard it. Anyway, I'm going back there tomorrow after school to take some pictures. Go with me, you guys. It would be so cool if we could sneak inside."

"No way!" Juniper said, flatly. "One sneeze and it might cave in. It's never really been a goal of mine to be buried in decay, you know. Oh yeah, and then there's that 'Danger—No Trespassing' sign by the front porch. I do believe that's more than just a warning."

"You're chicken," Anne said, hoping some name calling would change Juniper's mind. Truth was, Anne was a bit chicken too. Why else ask Juniper and Gena to tag along?

"Then call me chicken too," Gena chimed in, "but not because I'm afraid the house might fall on top of me. I'm not one to disturb a ghostly presence. Especially in its own territory."

"You're scared we'll find the Gray Lady?" Anne blurted with a giggle.

"Not exactly," Gena answered. "I'm more afraid that *she* will find *us!*"

⋆ ⋆ ⋆

Anne carried her camera to school so she'd have it handy when she went back to Boogerman's house. After classes, she pedaled straight up to the iron fence, and as quiet and cautious as possible, opened the squeaky gate. *Just a few feet or so inside the yard won't hurt anything.* She wasted no time, snapping one picture after another—kneeling, leaning, taking vertical shots, horizontal ones—every possible angle. She took pictures of the doors, windows, and the historical marker planted firmly by the enormous front porch.

The Davis Home
Built 1881 by Carlton Davis
Prominent Avery Founder and Citizen

The two-story Victorian-style house at 701 Shady Lane hadn't seen a speck of paint in a hundred years. Its shutters were either snaggle-toothed or missing, and its gables leaned off-kilter. Anne stared at the house, mesmerized. The house appeared to be staring back.

Then she dared to venture around to the back, careful to step over a few broken bottles. Anne had never been this close to the house, or seen the back. It looked more peaceful and cozy back here. A wild rose garden covered the back fence, or maybe it should be called a wild rose jungle. A gang of skinny cats roamed through it, and Anne figured they must be strays. They didn't look like typical, plump, domestic housecats.

The trees back here were gigantic and probably older than science. They thoroughly shaded the ground, which consisted of dirt rather than grass.

The house definitely seemed older from this view. There was a rusted-out bucket on the back porch—a small rickety porch that leaned slightly toward two rows of corroded pipes that outlined one side of the backdoor. The pipes took a sharp left just above it, disappearing into a square hole.

Something hissed, sending Anne out of her skin. *Phew! Just one of the cats.* He arched his back at her. She snapped more pictures, including one of that crabby cat, then left. *Strange.* She wasn't frightened of the place at all. Not like when she was little. But suddenly, while riding away, she got an odd feeling. Someone was watching her. More than watching–inspecting her. *Silly.* Old houses probably gave everyone that chilling feel.

⋆ ⋆ ⋆

Once she was home, Anne put the camera away.

"How did the photo session go?" Mom asked, cutting a slice of spice cake and setting it before Anne.

"It went okay," Anne answered. The cake went down moist and tasty, just like all of Mom's baking. "I wish you'd lived on this side of town when you were a little girl," she said. "You'd probably have some great stories to tell me about that place."

"I wouldn't have gone anywhere near it," Mom said. "Not even on a dare. You're much braver than I am."

That got Anne to thinking. *I wonder how many people* did *go there on a dare?*

"It'll be fun to research that old place though. There are lots of people around here who've lived near it all their lives. I bet you'll find one or two to talk to."

Anne knew she would. She almost wished she didn't have other homework assignments. She wanted to focus full-time on the history of Boogerman's house and its famous ghost, the Gray Lady.

Once she'd eaten her cake, drank a glass of milk, and wiped the moo juice from her upper lip, she went to the computer to download the pictures. She plugged in the camera, then sat, eyeing each one closely. *Good job, Donovan!* she thought. *This was some great photography, even if I say so myself.* But then, there were no people in them to blink or sneeze or move about, causing a major blur. And better still, her thumb hadn't found its way in front of the lens, and neither had her hair, on any of the pictures. *Awesome.*

Although the house was ramshackle and worse for wear, the pictures she took were vibrantly colored. The trees, the roses, even the smoky color of the bare wooden frame was alive. *These are going to go great with my research project!*

Anne was about to save them all and click print when something in one of the pictures caught her eye. She moved in closer to see. *What was that?* She enlarged the image for an even better inspection, then quickly jumped back. *Holy ghosties!* Anne got up and walked in a circle for a moment, trying to compose herself. Her thoughts raced. She grabbed the phone and dialed Juniper.

Juniper had barely said hello when Anne blurted, "Call Gena, quick. Both of you get over here . . . now!"

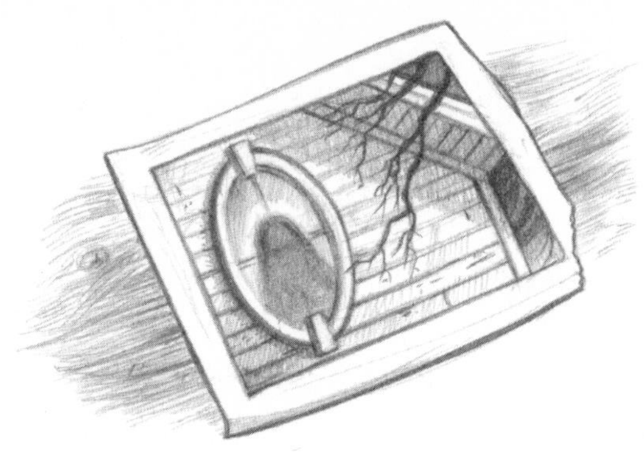

CHAPTER 2

The Blob

The three girls hovered over Anne's computer, oohing and ahhing at the digital photos.

"I've got to admit," Gena said, "You've really got guts!"

Juniper nodded. "I'd never go into Boogerman's backyard by myself."

"I didn't mean that," Gena said. "I'm talking about how brave she was to use this fancy camera. My pictures never come out."

Anne rolled her eyes. "Maybe you should try taking the lens cover off."

Juniper laughed as Anne clicked on another computer image. "Here's the one I wanted you guys to see." They leaned in.

The picture showed the back of Boogerman's house, looking grayer and more dilapidated than ever. The afternoon sun reflected off all the windows but one. "Right there," Anne said, pointing to a little attic window. "What's that?"

She watched as Juniper and Gena squinted toward it. She could practically see their wheels turning, trying to decipher the weird gray blob inside that window.

"It looks like somebody smeared the picture with a dirty eraser," Gena said. "Are you trying to trick us or something?"

"Nobody tried to erase or tamper with the picture," Anne argued. "And besides, wouldn't the smears be on the outside of the window too? Look. The gray thingy stops at the window frame." *How could Gena not see what she was seeing?*

"What do you think it is?" Juniper asked. "'Cause it just looks like a glitch in the film to me."

"Look now," Anne said. She clicked on *zoom,* framing the blob in a much bigger format. Juniper and Gena both popped back.

Gena's mouth dropped. "Is that a face?" she asked.

Anne sighed. "Thank you! I was hoping I wasn't the only one seeing it."

"It looks so creepy," Juniper said, displaying an exaggerated shiver. "Heck, you can't even tell if it's a man or a woman."

Anne agreed. Just two eyes and a mouth. No hair or other facial features to distinguish it as male or female. Just a face peeping out of a fog. It gave her a serious case of the willies. "But it is definitely human," she said. "Do you know what this means?"

"That you'll get an A+ on your report?" Gena said.

"No! I'm probably the first person ever to catch the Gray Lady on film. I mean, who else could that be?"

Juniper held up her hand, shaking her head. "It might not be anybody. It could be some trick of the light or the angle. Remember the face on Mars?"

"Like the man in the moon?" Gena asked.

Juniper nodded. "Kind of. A few years ago they sent a spacecraft to Mars to take pictures. One picture showed a rock with a face on it. People started saying that it had been carved that way, and it meant there was either an ancient civilization that once lived there, or that someone had gone there in a rocket a long time ago and carved it then. Anyway, later on, they got another picture of the rock from a different angle, and it turned out to be just a craggy old rock. It was the shadows that had made the rock look like it had a face."

"But this is different," Anne said. "The face in this picture couldn't be formed from shadows. Look at the eyes and mouth. They're practically white. Wouldn't a shadow make them darker?"

Juniper and Gena both looked toward her, their faces as blank as a power outage. "We could sit here and guess at this all night," Juniper said. "But it would probably be better to double-check."

"How?" Anne had always double-checked her resources for her reports in the past, but how do you double-check a ghost?

"Go back and take some more pictures," Gena said. "See if it shows up again."

"This could be a once-in-a-lifetime thing," Anne said. "What are the odds of her showing her face at the window again while I'm taking pictures?"

Juniper tapped the camera with her finger. "Why not take it to an expert, like someone at a film place? They can tell shadows from real stuff. That's how they found out those pictures of Bigfoot and the Loch Ness Monster weren't real."

Anne's spirits sank. "Experts? Believe me, no one at the Photo Hut would know the difference. Where do I find an expert on ghosts?"

Gena slumped into a chair. "Oh man, this is terrible."

"I know," Anne said. "How am I going to prove this?"

Gena crossed her arms, pouting. "Not that. I can't believe those weren't real pictures of Bigfoot and Nessie!"

Anne slung the mouse pad at her.

* * *

The Fortune Tellers Club gathered under the patio area of the school. The rain pounded on the metal roof, preventing them from hanging out at their usual spot under the magnolia tree.

"Guess you won't be taking pictures today," Gena said, pointing skyward.

Anne smiled. "That's okay. I'm doing something better. Research."

"At the public library?" Juniper asked. "Because I'm going there this afternoon to find more info on the Lincoln Memorial. The school library doesn't have enough books about it."

"Not today," Anne said, disappointed. "I'm going to research it a little differently. I was really hoping you guys could come along. I'm planning to talk to someone who grew up around Boogerman's house."

"Who?" Gena asked.

Anne shrugged. "I don't know yet. Mom says there's some really nice people who attend her church that would probably talk to me. Want to come with me, Gena?"

"Sure," Gena said. "That beats what I was going to do."

"What?" Anne and Juniper asked together.

Gena smiled. "I was going to go with Juniper to the library to research 'Our Four Fathers.'"

"Then I suggest you keep your original plans," Juniper said. "This is not like those book reports you can do the night before, you know. Remember, the bibliography has to contain more than just internet sites."

Gena slumped and moaned. "You're on your own, Anne."

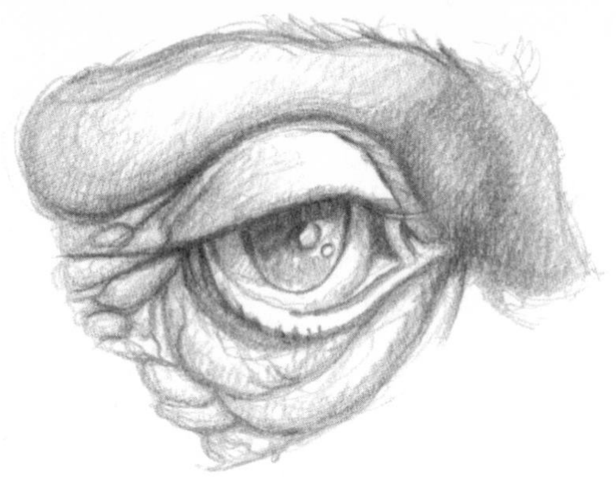

CHAPTER 3

Revisiting the Past

Anne pedaled her bike on the rain-slicke streets, a small tape recorder, pencil, and paper in her backpack. She also had a couple of names and addresses her mother had given her before she'd left. She was going to visit Mrs. Draper first. Mom said that Mrs. Draper was older than God and had lived around here before the dawn of time. Scanning the names and numbers on the mailboxes, Anne hoped the address she needed would be easy to find. She finally found it, sitting alone on the corner, one long block from Boogerman's house.

She double-checked the address then strolled up onto a small porch, bumping her head on a small dangling wind chime, thin as a spider's web. She knocked on the door, then knocked again. *Bummer! Guess she's not home.* Anne was about to turn away when a teeny woman with thin white hair answered the door.

"Hi," Anne said, trying not to stare. It certainly wasn't the first time she'd seen an elderly person, but Mrs. Draper looked like she hadn't been in the sun for at least a decade. Her face and hands were freckled in brown splotches, and her eyes were like wee dots of milk.

"Who are you?" Mrs. Draper asked, her voice soft and raspy.

"My name is Anne. I'm Carolyn Donovan's daughter."

"Who?" Mrs. Draper asked a little louder.

Anne raised her voice too. "Mrs. Donovan's daughter. I think you know my mom from church."

"Oh, yes, Carolyn. She brings those butter roll pastries to the potluck on Wednesday nights."

"That's her," Anne said. "I was wondering if I could ask you some questions?"

"Come in."

As Mrs. Draper shuffled down the hall, Anne couldn't help but think she looked like a tiny bobbing shrimp.

Anne followed, mesmerized by the house inside. It looked more like a museum than a residence, decorated with old portraits, china candy dishes, and lace doilies on just about everything. The whole place smelled of menthol and talcum powder. She accidentally bumped against a floor lamp, jiggling the crystals that hung from the bottom of the shade.

Mrs. Draper led her past the living room, and continued into the kitchen, where she took a seat at a dining table. Anne figured this must be Mrs. Draper's "nest." The chair had pillows, and faced a small TV on a corner shelf. Just above was a parakeet, twitting and chirping in a rusted birdcage. Anne sat down at the end of the table.

"My mom says you've lived here all your life."

"All my eighty-four years, honey," Mrs. Draper said, her voice labored with valleys and peaks.

"I'd like to know about the house at 701 Shady Lane." Anne searched Mrs. Draper's eyes for a reaction. There was none. She just blinked and smiled.

"That old place? Ain't nobody lived there since I can remember."

"What can you remember?" Anne desperately wanted to know.

"Not much."

Anne realized this wasn't going to be easy. Her mom would have said it was like pulling teeth. But Mrs. Draper didn't look as though she had many teeth left to pull.

"Do you know about the Gray Lady?"

This time Mrs. Draper's eyes did show a reaction. "Are kids still talking about her? I'll swear."

Anne nodded, then a silence stretched between them. She felt oddly uncomfortable asking to record the visit, but finally unzipped her backpack, taking out the tape recorder. "I'm doing a report on the house, and I'd like you to fill me in about some things if you could."

"I'll try, but my memory isn't much good anymore."

Anne smiled, hoping that would help. "Any information would really help me a lot." She clicked the record button and set the small tape recorder on the table. "What can you tell me about that house?"

Mrs. Draper tilted her head in thought. "Besides the haunted stuff, you mean?"

"Anything," Anne urged.

"I don't know much about it. The man who built it was a banker, I think? But his wife was a bit loco. Hanged herself in the attic. That's whose ghost is gallivanting around there."

Anne shrugged off a chill. "So you believe in the Gray Lady?" Anne asked, suddenly more anxious for answers.

"Oh goodness, I don't know. You should probably ask Wilbur Nicholson. He's the one who claimed to see her."

Anne recognized the name. He was on the list her mom had given her. "But you've never seen the Gray Lady?" Anne continued.

"Never," Mrs. Draper said, her eyes twittering like the parakeet above her.

Anne wondered if Mrs. Draper was holding something back, consciously or subconsciously. "Have you seen or heard anything inside that house?"

"I'm sorry, honey," Mrs. Draper said. "I guess I'm just no use to you. You really should ask Wilbur, though. He probably doesn't want me blabbing it, but he got arrested for mischief in that house." She slapped her hand on the table as she said it, causing the parakeet to flutter frantically.

"What did he do to get arrested?" She didn't think she'd have the nerve to ask Mr. Nicholson herself.

"Oh, dear. It was just silly child's play. And it was so long ago."

"Please tell me," Anne said.

Mrs. Draper folded her hands in front of her. "He and some of the neighbor boys went in on a dare. They did that sort of thing in my day. Silly, when you think about it. Wilbur claimed the other boys were just tricking him, and they slipped away, leaving him there all alone. He says he climbed the stairs up to the attic, and he saw the lady hanging from her noose. Then she fell to the floor, got up, and started chasing him. He broke a window getting out, even cut his arm. The police arrested him for vandalism." Mrs. Draper shook her head. "Of course, they didn't believe his ghost-chasing story."

Anne swallowed, noticing her throat had become dry. "Do *you* believe it?"

"Wilbur believed it," Mrs. Draper said. "He wouldn't set foot anywhere near that house again—not even on the same street. He sure did scare us with that story."

Anne leaned back in her chair. "Maybe I *will* talk to him. Is there anything else you can tell me?"

Mrs. Draper's eyes suddenly cleared. She smiled like a small child. "There used to be this silly rhyme we'd say. Goodness! Until now, I hadn't thought of it in years and years." She turned toward Anne a bit more, leaning in. Her voice low and hypnotic. *"Don't go near old Boogerman's house or goblin bells will toll. 'Cause Boogerman's just the Devil himself and he'll swallow you up whole."*

Anne's entire body flared in goose bumps, and suddenly she wanted to leave. She needed details, yes . . . but not a poem that scared the willies out of her. "Thanks," she said, finding it hard to speak. Clicking off the recorder, she grabbed it, put it in her backpack, and stood. "Bye. Uh . . . and thanks."

"Come again," Mrs. Draper said.

Don't count on it, Anne thought, as she forced a nervous smile. Hopefully, the rest of the research wouldn't be this eerie.

CHAPTER 4

The Cards Never Lie

"Wow, they called it Boogerman's house way back then?" Gena asked, popping a handful of M&Ms in her mouth.

"Obviously," Anne said, still suffering from the willies. "But it's not so much the rhyme as the way she said it. It spooked me big time! Listen." She rewound the tape recorder for just a second, then played Mrs. Draper reciting the rhyme.

Gena gasped and held up her hands. "It's official. I am now totally weirded out."

Juniper grabbed the giant M&M bag and scooped some out. "I think it's awesome." She reached over and picked up the photo Anne had taken of the attic window. "Why didn't you show her the picture?"

"What good would that do?" Anne said. What if she *had* shown Mrs. Draper the photo? Would Mrs. Draper have freaked out or laughed?

Juniper munched her candy while talking. "She might have recognized the face."

"But we don't know if it really is a face," Anne said. "It may just be a photo glitch. Most likely . . . right?" But secretly, Anne knew the true question was: *Who was that looking out? The Gray Lady or Boogerman himself?* She shivered again, then tried to mentally convince herself it really was a glitch.

Gena examined the photo and shrugged. "It's certainly not the window cleaner. You can see the cobwebs on the corners of the window."

Anne froze, absorbing Gena's words. "You're right!" She took the picture back for a closer look. "You can see the cobwebs. And they are in front of the gray blob." She dropped it on the floor where they sat. "Have you ever heard of a glitch *behind* the objects in a photo?"

"Seriously," Juniper said. "You need to go online and find someone who can analyze that picture. If it's legit, you have so much more than a book report here."

"Yeah!" Gena blurted, bouncing excitedly and scattering M&Ms. "And you'll get rich!"

Anne just stared. "What?"

"Do you know how much the *National Enquirer* would pay for a picture of a real ghost? Wow! Think of the things you could buy us!"

"Shut up," Anne said, picking up some of the M&Ms and chucking them at Gena. "I have a better idea."

"What?" Juniper asked.

Anne paused, wondering if she really should suggest it. "We should go inside Boogerman's house and investigate for ourselves."

Gena coughed, sputtering like the candy had caught in her throat. "By *we* you do mean *you,* right?"

"No. By *we* I mean *us.*"

Gena shook her head and held up her hands. "Not me! I'm not ringing any goblin bells. And I sure don't want to be swallowed up by the Boogerman."

"I'm not worried about Boogerman," Juniper said, "but I am worried about the Gray Lady."

"Oh yeah," Gena added, "and the fact that that old decrepit house itself is about to come tumbling down. Remember, Juniper? On your head!"

"You're right," Juniper said. "It could be really dangerous."

Anne desperately wanted to convince them. She had always been mesmerized by that house, and now, no matter how scary, she felt the need to check it out inside. It wasn't about the report anymore. It was solely about the mystery. "You guys are sooooooo chicken."

Gena cleared her throat of the dregs of M&Ms. "Why did the chicken cross the road?"

Anne sighed, "I don't know."

"To get away from Boogerman's house. Yes, Anne, I'm chicken."

Anne noticed Juniper had been especially silent, staring at the picture. "What about you? You won't go in?"

"I'm not sure. I think I want some reassurance before going inside."

"What kind of reassurance?" Anne asked. "It's not like someone is going to roll out the red carpet for us."

Juniper smiled. "No, but we could get some psychic reassurance."

Gena threw an M&M in the air and caught it in her mouth. "I guess this meeting of the Fortune Tellers Club has officially begun."

Anne dug through her divination tools and pulled out the deck of fortune telling cards that she'd bought the last time she'd been to the Village. They were small and cutesy, but the answers were in plain English so there was no real guess work involved. "These should be fun. They were designed mostly to answer questions."

She shuffled them like a regular deck of cards. "What should we ask?"

Gena scooted in, pushing the candy bag out of their circle. "Is the photo a fake?"

Anne turned up a card showing a picture of a gaunt face with one tear suspended from an eye. Inside the tear were the words *It isn't likely.*

"Whoa! Those cards are awesome!" Gena said.

Juniper grinned. "The picture looks sad, but it answered the question. It isn't likely that the photo is a fake."

Anne felt the chills coming on again. She hadn't known for sure if the ghost in the picture was real, but reconfirming it was scary. "Next question?"

"My turn," Gena said. "Does Boogerman really live in that house?"

Anne flipped a card over. It showed a hand holding a magnifying glass. Magnified under the glass were the words *I doubt it.*

Juniper let out a large sigh. "That should put your mind at ease."

"How?" Gena asked. "It didn't say no."

Anne shuffled the cards again. "Now let *me* ask a question. Should we go inside and investigate the house?" She turned the card over slowly this time. It showed a fluffy cloud with golden gates opened in its center, and a stream of water running through. A banner hung above the gates, reading *The channel is open.*

"That's freaky," Juniper said.

Anne didn't say anything. She picked it up and shuffled again. She shut her eyes to help her concentrate. "Is the Gray Lady inside Boogerman's house?"

The card showed flowers raining from a pink sky. *It's possible.*

She shuffled furiously now. "Will we be in danger if we go in?"

The card showed a box covered in dust. A key hung above the box with a tag that said *The hidden shall reveal itself.*

"Can I ask something?" Gena said.

Anne ignored her, still shuffling and thinking. "Will I find what I'm looking for there?"

The card showed an ancient man, sitting crosslegged on a flying carpet. *Consult the wise.*

"Well, that settles it then," Juniper said. "You should consult someone who knows something about photography."

Anne thought hard. That wasn't the question she'd asked. *Consult the wise? Who?* She hadn't told Juniper and Gena about Mrs. Draper's suggestion to speak to Mr. Nicholson, but he *had* been inside that house. He claimed to have seen the ghost. Heck, he claimed to have been terrorized by the ghost! Of course it could have been a prank. Still feeling edgy, Anne decided she'd have to talk to Wilbur Nicholson, but she didn't want to do it alone. She wanted her friends with her.

"So?" Gena asked. "Do you know *anyone* who does photography?"

Anne gave her a slight shrug. "I could probably find someone." She knew she'd end up talking to Mr. Nicholson, but it would probably be best to authenticate that photo first. But what if it was real? What would happen if she showed it to him?

CHAPTER 5

Change of Plans

Anne hurried over to the magnolia tree behind the school to hang out with Juniper and Gena before the bell rang. She'd barely made it there when Beth Wilson came scampering over, waving her arms and shouting, "Anne! Anne!" Nicole Hoffman trotted behind her.

"Anne! Omigosh! We've got a major emergency. I'm talking the ultimate S.O.S." Beth panted like she'd just lost a relay race.

"What, you forgot your cherry yum-yum lip gloss?" Gena said, cocking her head to the side.

Beth gave her a dragon stare. "Excuse me, is your name Anne?"

"There is no excuse for you," Gena said, snickering.

"What's the emergency?" Anne asked, wanting to get this over with. She had too much on her mind to deal with Anne and Gena's ongoing feud with the Snotty Twins.

"My mom can't take us tomorrow to get the braids!"

Anne stared, trying to comprehend.

"The braids?" Beth continued. "Remember? We decided last week that we'd all wear those neon braids for that special cheer routine we're doing at the pep rally. I promised to go this weekend to pick them up, and now I can't. The oil light keeps coming on in my mom's car, and she can't get it fixed until Monday. So do you think your mom could take us?"

Anne sighed. The braids were a fun idea, but she had more immediate plans. "Can't Nicole's mom take you?"

Beth looked genuinely puzzled. "Nicole's not even a cheerleader. Why would her mom take us?"

Juniper stepped forward. "But Nicole is going with you, right?"

"Nobody asked you," Nicole said, wrinkling her nose.

Juniper held up her hand and backed away. "Just asking."

"Oh, go poke a voodoo doll or something," Beth snapped.

Anne quickly cut in. "I can ask my mom when I get home. I'm sure she'll take us."

Beth beamed. "I knew we could count on you, Anne."

"But where are we going to buy them?"

"That's the best part!" Beth squealed. "There's a new place in the Village that has all kinds of strange costumes and stuff. They have loads of hair pieces in every color you can imagine."

"I'm imagining puke green," Gena said. "Bet that color would look great on you."

"Every color looks great on me," Beth smirked. "Except that icky color you're wearing in your hair."

Gena narrowed her eyes. "I'm not wearing a hair piece."

Beth looked at Gena like she was carrying a disease. "Ew! That's really your hair?"

She and Nicole darted away, giggling. "Call me after you ask your mom," she yelled back.

"Those two should really consider having themselves surgically separated," Juniper said.

Gena laughed. "And Beth should go in for an ego reduction."

Anne didn't want to hear it. She had an obligation to the cheerleaders, and knew she'd end up spending the day with Beth and Nicole instead of investigating the house like she'd planned. The bell rang, and she hurried ahead of Juniper and Gena into the school.

* * *

Anne sat in the front of the station wagon next to her mom. Beth and Nicole chattered in the back—mostly about boys and clothes, but Nicole did manage to get in a few digs about dance, bragging on about being the best at her studio. Anne knew better. Nicole was good, but Juniper had always been able to dance rings around her. Anne didn't talk much. She kept thinking about her social studies report. She'd been dwelling too much on the legends, and not on the history of the house. Maybe she should forget the photo and any firsthand account of spooks. She needed to know more about the house itself.

When they reached the Village, her mom turned off the main road. Anne had never been to this section. It looked more like a narrow alleyway than a road, and the shops were tiny and obscure. Mom pulled over and parked at the curb, right in front of the Enchanted Wardrobe—one bizarre-looking store. The window dressing spoke for it, displaying everything from wild tee shirts to belly-dance attire. Anne had no doubt this shop would have neon hair braids.

Beth and Nicole jumped out, giggling and racing into the store.

"I'll wait here," Mom said, as Anne opened the door. Anne didn't argue. She knew her mom wouldn't go into a store like this, even if it was Halloween. She smiled. "We'll try not to be too long."

Anne ran in, catching up with Beth and Nicole who were oohing and ahhing over a display of Mardi Gras masks. "Wow!" Beth said, picking one up and placing it over her eyes. "I love the peacock feathers!"

"I like this one." Nicole modeled a mask with white sequins and black willowy feathers.

Beth stomped her foot. "Oh, we should have thought about using masks for the pep rally routine. It would have looked so cool."

Anne agreed. She would definitely have chosen the iridescent turquoise with the purple plumes. "But we came here for braids, so let's find them."

Beth moaned and they browsed along, stopping at the vintage clothing, jewelry, and tiaras . . . tiaras! "Don't I look totally regal?" Beth asked.

"Major coolio!" Nicole replied.

Anne took a deep breath. "Braids. Let's find the braids."

The braids were with the other hair accessories on the back wall. Boy, Beth wasn't kidding when she said this place had a huge variety—every color imaginable, even some colors Anne had never seen, much less imagined. They picked out the wildest colors for the cheer squad.

"Choose the color you want, Anne," Beth said. "I'm going to wear the fuchsia. We'll let the rest of the team fight over the rest."

Anne shrugged. "I'll decide in the car on the way home." As they stepped up to the checkout counter, Anne happened to look up and out of the window. Directly across the street was a teeny shop with a small window displayed with photos. A sign above the door read *The Darkroom—Extreme Photography*. Maybe this day wouldn't be a washout after all.

CHAPTER 6

The Darkroom

Beth and Nicole became preoccupied with the oddities in the counter display case, and since Beth held the money to pay for the braids, Anne tapped her on the shoulder. "I'm going over *there* for a minute." She pointed out the window.

Beth never looked up. "Whatever."

Anne rushed out the door, and ran around to the driver's side of Mom's car. "I'm just going to run into that photo shop. I won't be long."

Mom looked up from the newspaper she was reading. She glanced at the shop and smiled. “Okay.” She went right back to the article Anne had pulled her from.

When Anne opened the shop’s door, she felt like Alice tumbling into Wonderland. The place was dark with the exception of several soft spotlights in the ceiling. Each light shone down on various portraits resting on easels.

Anne stepped up to the nearest picture. She was shocked to see that it wasn’t a painting, as she expected, but a photograph—an extremely bizarre photograph. That’s why this place is labeled *Extreme Photography!* She took a minute to absorb the image. The photo was of a young woman wearing a pale green Grecian gown with bright, white, feathered wings. She was lying on a cloud, looking down at a road filled with street performers—jugglers, puppeteers, mimes. The woman in the picture, whom Anne assumed represented an angel, was tossing down teeny numbers, musical notes, and smiles. The smiles were real human lips. The label under the photograph said *The Beggar’s Muse.* Anne loved it.

Centered in the next spotlight was a much smaller picture of a merry-go-round in the middle of a playground. At least Anne thought it was a playground. It was hard to tell since the merry-go-round was standing still, and the park around it was blurred from spinning. The visual effect was awesome! She saw that this picture was titled *Still Life*.

As she sauntered to the next picture, a short man in baggy jeans and a tee shirt came out of a back room. "Can I help you with something?"

"Do you work here?" Anne asked.

The man smiled, his mustache spreading to his dimples. "You can say that."

Anne couldn't contain her excitement over the pictures in the gallery. She only wished Juniper and Gena were here to see them. "These are great! Do you know the photographer?"

"Yes, I do," the man answered. "Are you thinking of purchasing one?"

"I wish," Anne said, feeling like a toddler in a toy store. "Are they expensive?"

The man blinked and nodded.

"Well, truthfully," Anne started, trying to pick her words carefully, "I'd like to have a word with him . . . the photographer."

The man crossed in front and cast his gaze on the portrait. He stroked his chin. "Is there something wrong with this picture?" Just as quickly he turned to Anne. "Or are you a budding photographer?"

"No, no!" Anne said, feeling silly. "There's definitely nothing wrong with that picture. And I'm hardly a photographer. But I bet he knows lots about photo glitches."

"That he does."

Anne felt antsy and anxious. *Enough small talk.* "Do you know where I can find him? I'd really like to ask him a question."

The man smiled again, spreading his mustache in an enormous grin. He extended his hand. "I took these pictures. I'm Jess Fallon."

Anne shook his hand, feeling a little awestruck. "Sorry. I thought you were a clerk or something."

"I get that all the time," he said, joking. "So what's your question?"

Anne wasn't sure how much to reveal. Mr. Fallon's photography was obviously painted with digital graphics, but would he be able to tell if something was real or fake? She thought about the "real" human smiles in the first picture. "I took a picture of a house. It's a vacant house, but in the photo someone is looking out one of the windows. It looks totally real, but I need to know if it is or isn't."

"Captured a ghost, huh?"

Anne must have revealed the answer with her eyes because Mr. Fallon chuckled. "A ghost doesn't have to be a real spirit. It could be a double exposure or a chemical imbalance in the film. Even the lighting can cause a ghost to appear in photos."

Anne nodded, a bit relieved. "Then yes, I've captured a ghost."

"Do you have the picture with you?"

Darn! Anne wished she did. "No, but I could arrange to come back and bring it."

Mr. Fallon nodded. "What type of film were you using?"

"I don't know," Anne said, shrugging. "It was my dad's digital camera."

"Well, in that case, we can make a different arrangement." He walked over to a skinny, white desk in the back corner of the room and turned on a lamp. Picking up a business card, he scribbled something on the back. "Here." He came back and handed it to Anne. "This is my email address. Do you know how to send a photo as an attachment?"

"Oh yeah!" Anne said, happy that this was going to be easier than she'd thought.

"Send it whenever you can."

Anne bounded to the door, feeling light as a helium balloon. "Oh, Mr. Fallon?"

"Uh huh?"

"Don't laugh at my photography."

He grinned and looked around his gallery. "Okay. As long as you promise not to laugh at mine."

CHAPTER 7

The Glow

Anne rushed out, hopped into the car, and strapped on the seatbelt. Beth and Nicole were already in the backseat.

"What were you doing in there?" Nicole asked.

Anne looked back over her shoulder. "Just checking on something."

Beth curled her lip in disapproval. "Doesn't look too exciting to me. Here, pick one." She opened the bag for Anne to choose which color braid she wanted as Mom started the car and drove away.

"Darn!" Nicole said, looking back. "Was that photographer looking for models?"

Beth snatched the bag away before Anne could get her hand out. "Oh, Nic! We should have gone in with Anne!" She slowly opened the bag again, but Anne could see both girls were pouting over missing their chance to be discovered as cover girls.

"I'll take the purple braid. And don't worry, he wasn't looking for models." She could only imagine their gagging at one of Jess Fallon's weird photos.

Although Beth and Nicole begged Anne to go with them to the mall, she honestly told them that she had some homework to do, particularly her social studies report. This didn't register well on their "nerdy meter," but Anne didn't care. Some kids went out of their way to meet with the approval of the Snotty Twins. Anne wasn't so superficial.

Once she got home, she went straight to the computer and pulled up the photo. She attached it to an email and wrote:

> Mr. Fallon,
>
> I'm the girl who met you at your store. Here's the photo I told you about. Any information you can give me would be greatly appreciated.
>
> Thanks!
> Anne

She clicked *send* and hoped he'd hurry with an answer. But how does an expert photographer know these things? Would he just look at it? Test it somehow? Maybe he had to print it out and run a chemical over it or something? Anne didn't have a clue. But she realized that it could take longer than she hoped.

She tried calling Juniper and Gena. Juniper's dad said she'd gone to the store with her mom, and she got Gena's goofy message on the Richmond's answering machine. Anne was too nervous and fidgety to sit and wait. She needed to do something to focus and keep her mind off the weird photo. She got her bike out of the garage and went riding. At least that's what she told herself. Going riding meant that . . . just riding, going no place in particular, but she knew the minute she pedaled down the street that no place in particular would end up being Boogerman's house.

She sailed past the well-groomed homes in her neighborhood. The day was sunny and bright with no sign of rain. The air still held some humidity, making the temperature feel a little warmer and her skin a little icky, but she didn't mind. The breeze from her bike cooled her. She turned out of her neighborhood and headed north, pedaling faster, and racing past taller trees and older mailboxes. When she got to Shady Lane, the road appeared dark and ancient. Her bike was like a time machine carrying her back a hundred years or more. *Shady Lane—no wonder it's called that.* The enormous trees lining the road blocked out the sunlight. Wet leaves and pine needles were still plastered to the ground from the recent rain. As Anne continued toward the house, she heard music drifting through trees–soft, low, piano music. She hit her brakes, taking a second to remember. Piano music? Ghost music? She listened closely. *No way!* The tinkling of the piano keys seemed distant, even though the house was now in view. A strong wind suddenly stirred, blowing more damp leaves from the trees. She could still hear the music in the wind. Then it stopped.

Anne stayed frozen, wondering whether to turn around or keep going. She took a moment to catch her breath. Just then she heard the blast of a car horn on another street. Its blare sounded pretty loud. Anne exhaled her fears. Piano? She remembered Mrs. Draper's wind chimes. *That's it. Just someone's wind chimes on the next street.* Surely if the car horn was that loud, then wind chimes could easily be heard. She buried her worries and went on.

The house looked bleak and swollen in the damp air. Anne got off of her bike and leaned it against the iron fence. The gate squeaked loudly as she went through, and she didn't bother latching it back. She just stood, staring at the front door. *Too Dangerous,* she thought. As much as she wanted to go inside, it made no sense. One fall and she'd be trapped. Her cries for help would not be heard. Her only hope would be someone seeing her bike against the fence. *Just too risky.*

She didn't hesitate a minute, heading straight to the back yard. The dirt was still wet. Not muddy, just sticky, like black snow. Anne walked carefully so she wouldn't slip. Her concern was not with mud or piano music or exploring the inside. She raised her eyes to the small attic window. No gray glob today. Just an ordinary window with crusty old glass and cobwebs.

She took a step back and shrugged. What did she expect? Did she really think she'd see a face looking out at her? She thought of Mrs. Draper's story. *The wife was a bit loco too. Hanged herself in the attic.* That thought prickled her skin. She hurried back around, intending to get the heck away from there. As she rounded the side the house, she saw something that revved up her heartbeat. Anne stood motionless.

A glow. A silver-blue glow like a mysterious ghost light . . . was floating inside the front window!

CHAPTER 8

You've Got Mail

Anne ran from the frightening glow toward the front gate, the soles of her shoes sticking on the tacky mud ground. In her panic, she had no time to think or rationalize what she saw. Just as she reached the fence, her sneakers gave way and she slipped, hitting head first against the iron bars of the gate. She rolled over, rubbing the spot just above her hairline. Sticky, like the mud. She looked at her fingers. Blood. She pulled herself up and unlatched the gate.

The right leg of her jeans was smeared with black muck, and she knew it'd only make a bigger mess to try and brush it away with her hand.

Her bike had fallen too, and the handlebars were tangled inside the bars of the fence. Anne furiously jiggled and turned them until her bike was free. As she stood it up and hopped on, her eyes strayed up to the front window. The glow was there, emitting from below the bottom sill. Her feet and adrenaline both pumped at hyperspeed, and she pedaled for her life. Several blocks away, she took a long, deep breath.

* * *

I could have picked any place to report on, Anne thought as she ran the bathtub with warm water. *No ghosts at the Washington Monument. Or the Seattle Space Needle.* She stepped into the soothing water, erasing some of the fear still rolling through her. *I could have done my report on the Alamo. The ghosts there don't hurt anyone.* She pictured Mr. Nicholson as a young boy, terrorized by the ghost of a woman with a noose hanging around her neck. Anne felt chills even in the warm water. She put a wet rag to her injured head. Luckily, it was just a small cut–nothing that needed stitches, she didn't think. Her hair would hide it from view.

She hurried through her mud cleaning process and toweled off as the grimy water swirled down the drain. After putting on a clean shirt and jeans, she headed to the computer and brought up her email.

The first was from Juniper.

> Hey! Check this out! www.historicalavery.org. It's a website by two women who are trying to reform the Avery Historical Society that died out about ten years ago. Click on Davis House when you get there. Call me after. I'll be home.
>
> J.

Anne clicked the link. Obviously, Avery was a town with quite a bit of history. She had at least a dozen cyber buttons to choose from. When she clicked Davis House, the first thing to appear was a picture of it. Not Boogerman's house, like she was used to seeing, unpainted and shabby, but the Davis House, sturdy and elegant. Even though the black-and-white photo was worn and faded, it was evident to Anne that the house was brightly painted, and the yard well groomed, likely blooming with a rainbow of colorful flowers.

Why would anyone in this cozy house hang herself?

She scrolled down and read.

The Davis House has long been one of Avery's most historic and legendary homes, built by Carlton Davis and his wife, Isabelle, one of Avery's first families of settlers. Carlton Davis prospered as founder and president of the Avery Security Bank and Trust. Isabelle Davis, an accomplished pianist, taught piano lessons to the area children until Mr. Davis's disappearance in 1898. Scandal struck Avery as the town concluded that Mr. Davis had left to start a new life with his longtime secretary, Kate Hitchcock. Mrs. Davis, unable to cope with her heartbreak, became a recluse, spending long hours at her piano. The house fell into disrepair.

In June 1904, while traveling down Shady Lane, Mr. Malcolm Fogg noticed an unusual swarming of flies near the upper windows of the home. Suspicious, he stopped to investigate. "The back attic window was thick with them," Mr. Fogg told reporters. "You could hear them buzzing like a saw."

Finding all the doors and windows locked, Mr. Fogg retrieved a ladder from the garage and climbed up to the attic window. Peering in, he saw Mrs. Davis's body hanging from a noose. The authorities ruled it a suicide.

Mrs. Davis's death left a stigma upon the house, leading to it's current condition. With the reformation of the historical society, the house can be refurbished and converted into a museum.

Anne sat back, absorbing the facts. *Wow! This is just what she needed for her report. Way to go, Juniper!* She pressed *print* and as the article came zipping out of the printer, she closed the site to look at the rest of her email. The next message was from Gena.

> Anne, I would ask where you are, but I'm guessing you're recovering from Snotty Twinitis. What's the latest on Boogerman?
>
> Gena

She didn't reply, just closed it out. It was the next email that made her heart yo-yo.

From: Shutterbug Fallon
Subject: Re: Photo Glitch

Anne's hand trembled as she slid the mouse and double-clicked. The first sentence zapped her breath.

> Looks like you've caught a real ghost!

CHAPTER 9

Ghost or Not?

Anne blinked and read on since this particular email meant everything.

There are experts far more skilled at photo analysis than I am, but for what it's worth, I studied your photo. Whatever that is in the picture, it is something tangent, meaning "real." It sort of looks like someone standing on the backside of a meat smoker or campfire, hidden behind a smoky cloud. I can see how it takes on a ghostly appearance, and I honestly believe the image is that of a woman.

By the way, isn't that the haunted house on Shady Lane? Did you take other photos as well? I wouldn't mind seeing them. Your angle on this one is great. I particularly like your perspective, meaning your focus on the area of the back of the house. Next time you're in the neighborhood, drop by with them. I can give you some free pointers on photography.

Good luck,
Jess Fallon

Anne couldn't help but beam a little about that last part, but she didn't have time to gloat about her photography skills. She grabbed the phone and called Juniper.

"I'm home," she said, when Juniper picked up. "I've got a lot to tell you!"

"I'll be right there," Juniper said.

"Wait! I'll call Gena. Bring your stuff to spend the night."

She looked at the photo one more time. Weird. The image in the window seemed stronger, more defined. Mr. Fallon was right. It did look like a woman.

* * *

It was over an hour later before Juniper came in, Gena stepping in behind her. They were confronted by Anne's mom as the three of them headed toward Anne's bedroom.

"Just in time," Mom said, wearing a warm smile. "I put some oatmeal cookies in the oven."

Anne wasn't interested in oatmeal cookies. She was about to explode from everything that had happened since that morning and couldn't wait to tell it all to the other Fortune Tellers Club members.

"Yum!" Gena said. "I love your oatmeal cookies, Mrs. Donovan. How long will they take before we can eat th—"

"We'll be in my room," Anne interrupted. They hurried back, and Anne closed the door.

Squatting in their usual circle, Anne poured out everything from the photography shop to the glow in the window to the article on the Davis House and finally, the email from Mr. Fallon. Juniper and Gena stopped her briefly with a question or two, but Anne pretty much controlled the conversation.

“So let me get this straight,” Gena said. “From what you’re telling us, someone is living in Boogerman’s house?”

“I’m not so sure about the *living* part,” Anne answered.

Juniper leaned forward, drawing little finger circles in the ivory carpet. “Do you really think it’s a ghost?”

Anne nodded. “It’s not like they don’t exist.”

“That’s true,” Juniper said. “But what now? Don’t you have enough for your report?”

Anne sighed. Did she? Probably. But it wasn’t about the grade anymore. She wasn’t sure it ever was. Her fun project had taken a major spin from a little snooping around to a full-blown spirit investigation–an investigation *she* was heading up. After today, she knew she couldn’t go back there alone, but she definitely needed to go back there. Mostly for her own sake. She had to know what was glowing in Boogerman's house.

"I say we go inside it," Anne told them.

The panic on Juniper's face said enough. Gena leaned toward her. "Anne, the report is on something *historical,* not *hysterical.* Which is what I'll be if you make me go into that haunted house." She grinned, batting her eyes.

"We'll be careful," Anne argued. "We'll take cell phones and whistles and any other emergency tools you guys can think of."

"Baseball bats?" Gena asked.

Juniper giggled. "Wouldn't a bat just swing right through a ghost?"

"No," Gena said. "The baseball bat would be to knock me unconscious when I start to die of fright."

"Gena's right, Anne. This would be dangerous. We told you that before."

Yes! Yes! Yes! Anne thought. "Can't you do it for *me?*" she pleaded. "I'll never ask another favor of either of you . . . ever, ever again."

"Not to mention you'd owe us big time," Juniper added.

"No way!" Gena shouted. "I'm not going in there."

The bedroom door opened, and Anne's mom came in with a plate of cookies. "Going in where?" she asked.

Thanks a lot, Gena! Anne thought fast. "The bathroom."

Mom looked puzzled, her eyebrows practically touching in the middle. "The bathroom?"

"Yeah, uh . . . Gena has to pee, but she won't go into the bathroom."

"Why not, Gena? That is the place to go when you have to pee."

Anne could see Juniper pinching her mouth closed. She was obviously stifling a massive giggle. Before Gena could answer, Anne shouted, "Bug! She saw a big hairy insect in there and now she's afraid to go."

"Well, for goodness' sake," Mom said, setting down the plate of cookies. She took off her shoe and headed back out the door. "I'll squash it."

The girls all slumped, Juniper spurting a wet, rolling laugh. Anne swatted Gena's arm. "Watch what you say."

"I didn't know she was coming in," Gena said, sounding defensive.

They waited, knowing Anne's mom would be back. It only took a minute. "I didn't see a bug, Gena. Was it a spider?"

Gena smiled at her sweetly. "Don't worry, Mrs. Donovan. It probably crawled down the drain."

"Okay. You can go to the bathroom now."

"I don't really have to go that bad," Gena said. "Thanks for the cookies."

Mom headed out, but Anne could still see a confused look on her face.

"Now," Anne said, breaking a cookie in half. "Hear me out. I'm not stupid. I know we run a risk going in there, mostly because it's old and dilapidated. But there *is* safety in numbers, as they say. All three of us could watch out for each other."

"Great," Gena said. "Then who'd be watching out for the Gray Lady?"

"Come on!" Anne said, sounding a little too whiney. "You've got to do this for me."

Juniper took a bite of her cookie, then wiped a sprinkling of crumbs off her shirt. "I've been thinking. Before we commit to going in Boogerman's house with you, why don't we pay a visit to that old guy first? The one you said got chased out by the ghost."

"Mr. Nicholson?" Anne said.

"Why not? Maybe he'll tell us something that would help us out before we walk into a trap."

Gena grabbed another cookie. "I'm for anything that keeps me from going into that spooky place."

Anne was still thinking. Juniper had a good point. Maybe she should talk to Mr. Nicholson first. And it'd be easier with the Fortune Tellers Club behind her. "All right," she agreed. "We'll go talk to him." She stood up, smoothing out her jeans.

“What’re you doing?” Gena asked.

“Going to talk to Mr. Nicholson.”

Gena’s mouth dropped, revealing a patch of crumbs plastered to her lip. “Right now?”

Anne looked at her watch. “It’s only 4:00. Let’s go.”

Juniper stood up and they both looked down at Gena.

“Okay, okay! I’m coming. But I really need to go to the bathroom first.”

As she walked away, Juniper called, “Watch out for big hairy insects!”

CHAPTER 10

The House of Charms

Again, Anne found herself on her bike, riding into the wind. This time, Gena and Juniper rode beside her. She paced her pedaling to stay next to them, mainly because she wasn't sure if she was really that anxious to talk to Mr. Nicholson. Did he see a gray haze, or a glow, or both? And if he did, were they just before being attacked by the ghost?

Anne's backpack was secured to her shoulders. Inside were the same tools she took to interview

Mrs. Draper—pen, paper, tape recorder, and some extra batteries. She had Mr. Nicholson's address scrunched up in her hand.

"So, does this guy live real close to Boogerman's house?" Gena asked, her voice trailing in the breeze.

"Weird, huh?" Anne said, her mind spinning at the thought.

Juniper glided a little closer. "What's so weird about it?"

Anne stared straight ahead as she answered. "Why would kids grow up and live in the same neighborhood? Don't people usually move away when they grow up and graduate and stuff?"

"Maybe they inherited their parents' houses," Juniper offered.

"Maybe they are cursed by a connection to Boogerman's house and are forced to live in an existence of never-ending fear," Gena said.

Anne nodded. "Maybe you're right."

Gena stopped pedaling, and drifted back a bit. "Maybe I was kidding!"

Anne took a sharp left three blocks from Boogerman's house. She looked at the paper crumpled in her hand: 719 Elm Street.

Like Mrs. Draper's street, two blocks away, the homes were mostly small, cracker-box-style houses, with the exception of a few made with dark, clay brick from the ground to the chimneys. Anne stopped in front of one. Without looking at the address, she knew it must be Mr. Nicholson's home. Like Mrs. Draper's home, there were wind chimes, but not just one set. Tinkling chimes hung from two trees in the front yard, two hung on the porch, and one set dangled from a long pole that was meant to hold a potted plant. Ivy ran wild across the ground, smothering most of the grass. The mailbox and front door both had horseshoes attached, open end up for good luck, and a small rippling fountain held a statue of four cherubs, each facing a different direction, aiming small arrows in their bows.

"This looks like the home of someone trying to ward off evil spirits, wouldn't you say?" Juniper said, stepping off her bike.

Anne didn't have to say. That had been her thoughts exactly. Gena had unknowingly been right.

"Is it just me, or do you guys find it more than creepy that he happens to live on Elm Street?" Gena asked.

Anne gave her a "get real" look rather than a reply.

Gena threw her hands up in surrender. "I'm just saying."

Juniper giggled. "Come on. We promise not to let Freddie Kruger do a number on you with his razor manicure."

"I don't know," Gena said. "This guy looks like he's trying to keep out something far more deadly than Freddie."

Anne wished Gena would hush. She was nervous enough as it was. "This guy goes to my mom's church. I don't think he'll jinx us or anything." Though she wasn't so sure. His yard did look like some massive hex to ward off the evil eye.

As they approached the door, Anne looked down at a pot of clover. Plain, old, regular, wild clover. Gena nudged her. "No doubt planted to sprout a bunch of the four-leaf variety." Anne nudged her back as she rang the doorbell.

No one spoke as they waited. Anne noticed Juniper fidgeting from one foot to the other. Gena was twisting the hem of her tee shirt into a giant knot with her finger. She stretched it so much that her pointer finger looked like a mummified hotdog. Anne tried to stay calm. Three jumpy girls would look a little strange to someone answering the door, and she didn't want to risk Mr. Nicholson turning them away. After a minute, Anne rang the bell again.

"Come on . . . answer," she heard Gena whisper under her breath. She figured Gena was worried about the consequences if no one was home. After all, if Mr. Nicholson didn't answer, Anne would insist they visit Boogerman's house on the way back. She knew she'd be able to convince them.

After another minute, she sighed. "Looks like no one's home. Let's go."

Juniper and Gena both looked deflated but a bit calmer too. “Maybe we can come back later,” Juniper said.

“Or call first,” Gena added quickly.

As they were stepping off the porch, a creaking noise made them turn back. The front door opened slowly. Standing there was a tiny boy with wisps of copper hair wearing nothing but a drooping Sesame Street diaper, grinning at them with itsy bitsy, pearl teeth.

“I got a motor boat!” He shouted. “Bbbbrrrrrrrrrrrrrrrrrrrrrrrr!” He held up a small, plastic boat for them to see, and made waving motions as he supplied the slobbery sound effects.

This was not at all what Anne expected. “Uh . . . do you live here?”

He giggled and added, “Brrrrrrrrrrrrrrrr!” dipping the boat through the waves of air. Suddenly, he was swept into the arms of a woman wearing brown pants and a pale, pink pullover. Her auburn hair looked a mess.

The Fortune Tellers Club took a step back when the woman approached them. She didn't say a word, but her knitted eyebrows were definitely inquisitive.

"Sorry to bother you," Anne said. "But we're here to speak with Mr. Nicholson. He goes to my mother's church."

The woman pushed a clump of hair behind her right ear. "My grandfather?"

The boy stopped doing a motorboat and chanted, "Poo Pa! Poo Pa! Poo Pa!"

"Yes," the woman said, setting the boy back on his feet. "They're here to see Poo Pa." She turned back to the girls as she scratched her nose with the back of her hand. "Let me see if he's awake."

She left the door open halfway and walked off. The little boy stood behind it, peeking around for a game of Peek-a-Boo. Gena leaned forward with her hands on her knees, "Do you know anything about our Four Fathers?"

The boy giggled. "Poo Pa!"

Juniper looked around Anne toward Gena. "Will you please give up on the four fathers nonsense! They are not our four fathers."

Gena sneered. "You're just jealous because I'm writing about four presidents and you're only writing about one."

"Stop," Anne whispered, seeing Juniper roll her eyes, preparing to say something back.

The woman returned, nodding. "He's awake. You can come in."

They followed her through a living room filled with oddly carved knickknacks and weird whatnots. Anne thought they looked a lot like the stuff you could buy at Pier 1 Imports. When Gena picked up a three-legged brass elephant, the woman noticed. "Grandpa was a world traveler. He collected art from the countries he visited. Most are from the African or Asian continent."

"This one's broken," Gena said, pointing to the missing leg.

The woman turned, leading them through a hallway and into a small, stuffy bedroom. By a desk sat a bald man with half-moon eyes and large ears. His hands trembled even though he was clasping the arms of the chair, and his nostrils flared with each breath he took.

“Try not to keep him too long,” the woman whispered. “His attention span suffers these days.” She left them alone with him.

Anne wished she’d rehearsed an opening ahead of time. How was she going to ask him about the Gray Lady? Before she could speak the man slowly raised a bushy, gray eyebrow.

“I know why you’re here,” he said. “You’ve seen her too.”

CHAPTER 11

Haunting the Past

Mr. Nicholson's statement caught Anne off guard. "Uh . . . we'd like to ask you some questions," she said.

He closed his half-moon eyes for a moment, then opened them wide. "Don't go near old Boogerman's house, or goblin bells will toll. 'Cause Boogerman's just the Devil himself and he'll swallow you up whole."

Anne shuffled back a step and glanced nervously at Gena. Gena's mouth had turned a chalky blue-white color. She turned to Juniper and noticed her face had gone pale too. “Mr. Nicholson?” Anne said, her voice cracking.

“You’ve seen her, haven’t you?” he said again.

“Just a picture of her.”

He suddenly perked up and gave her a thin, crooked smile. “Caught her on film, huh? Now that’s something I thought would never happen.”

Anne glanced at Juniper and Gena again, then said, “I’d like to know what happened the night you saw her. It’s for a school report. And can I record it on my tape recorder?” She reached into her backpack for it.

“Yeah,” he said, nodding. “I’ll tell you what I saw.”

Anne set the recorder on the desk by him. “Start at the beginning.”

“You girls might want to take a seat there.”

The three of them sat on the edge of the bed. Anne never took her gaze from Mr. Nicholson.

“It was so long ago, you’d think it might eventually fade. ’Course, I always prayed it would. But I can still see her as clearly as I see you.” He pointed a knobby, trembling finger at her.

Anne looked at his eyes with their half-closed lids. She wondered how clearly he really could see.

"I've been all around the world," he continued. "I've seen men in India walk on fiery coals, Haitians summon Voodoo magic, and a man levitate himself five inches off the ground while standing up. But nothing compares to her . . . the Gray Lady."

Anne heard Gena suck in a shaky breath. She realized they were all a bit rattled. But this was so important to her . . . or her report, she kept telling herself.

"It was hot that summer," Mr. Nicholson said. "July. A real scorcher. I was only eleven at the time. I ran with a couple of boys named Buddy and Sal. They were a little older and only let me hang around 'cause I was their gofer. 'Wilbur, gofer some ice cream for us.' 'Wilbur, gofer the baseball, it flew over the fence again.' Anything they asked for, I'd go for it. I really looked up to those two.

"So on that hot July night, when Sal said we should spend the night in Boogerman's house, I almost lied and told them I was sick. Nothing was going to get me inside that house. But Buddy said he'd read in the paper that there was a one-hundred-dollar reward for anyone who could stay there overnight—from dusk 'till dawn. He and Sal said we'd split the reward three ways. That money was so tempting to me. And I figured we'd be safe if there were three of us. We'd be able to look out for each other."

Anne absorbed every word. Particularly the last part. She knew his friends would betray him. *How sad.* She felt blessed to have two best friends who would stay beside her, even if it scared the snot out of them, like right now.

Mr. Nicholson lowered his head, then peered their way. Anne wondered if his attention span was suffering as his daughter had said. Finally, he began again.

"About eight o'clock—that's when the sun was just setting behind that house—we slipped around and snuck in the back way. Nobody would see. Right then I wondered why we were doing that. I asked Buddy, 'Don't we need some kind of witness that we spent the night here?

How are we going to prove we did it so we can collect the reward?' Buddy just snickered, then said, 'There's three of us, ain't there? We're our own witnesses.' I had no reason to doubt him.

"Now the backdoor went into the kitchen, see, and Sal jimmied the lock with a piece of copper wire. We had no problem getting in. We each had a flashlight, but Buddy was the only one to turn his on. We decided to take turns to save the batteries.

"Now, I figured we'd sit up all night by the backdoor and not bother with the rest of the house. But Buddy said the rules were, you only collected the reward if you stayed in the attic. I felt my stomach turn over about a dozen times. That money didn't sound so rewarding anymore. I knew I was stuck though. I couldn't let them think I was a baby. So I followed those two right up to the attic door."

Anne watched his expression change. His gaze became distant, as though his mind were reliving each moment.

"Funny thing about that door–it was small . . . even for a kid. I held the flashlight while Buddy and Sal pushed at it. They both had to push hard just to get it opened. I guess the wood had swollen from the heat and humidity. That July heat was the devil that year.

"As Buddy and Sal went in, Sal grabbed my arm, jerking me in with them. I shined the flashlight around the room. Just a large empty attic. The floor had been painted a steel gray color, and some of the paint was chipping. Over on the far wall was a small window, clouded with dust. I shined the light up at the ceiling. You could see clear up to the rafters. And there near the middle, was a couple of crossbeams, and a small piece of frayed rope tied to it. It looked like someone had sawed it short with a knife. Just seeing that made me want to turn and hightail it. I started backing toward the door when I heard it slam. I ran and jiggled the knob, but it was shut tight."

Mr. Nicholson rubbed his forehead again, this time like someone with a headache. His chest expanded and deflated as he took in a giant breath. Anne could hear the air rattle inside him. He cleared his throat.

"I sat down on the floor, trying not to cry. Not only was I scared, but I felt like a dang idiot. I knew those boys had played me for a fool, and if I hadn't been so terrified, I might have been humiliated. But I sat still, thinking about how I could get out. I went over to the window and tried to look out. The night was like pitch, and I couldn't see a thing. I was thinking that if I could get out that way, I might shimmy down from the roof. It was during that contemplating that I heard the noise. It was a squeaking sound that I thought was probably a mouse. But there is no such thing as a mouse that has a swaying rhythm to its squeak. I turned and shined the flashlight toward the noise."

His eyes grew twice their size, and Anne became aware that she'd been holding her breath. She let it out in a long, choppy wave.

"She was there. Dangling from a noose tied to the crossbeam—swinging slowly back and forth. Her head lobbed to the side like she was resting it on her right shoulder. Her eyes bulged, and her mouth hung open, exposing her black tongue. I was petrified, not able to move a muscle. The only noises were the creaking of that rope and the thudding of my heart. I thought I might die of shear terror. But the frightening part hadn't even come yet.

"My mind raced, trying to figure how to get out. I tried to open the window, but it was also swollen shut. When I turned back I flashed the light on her again. Her eyes clamped shut like I was blinding her. Then she raised her head straight up and opened her eyes again. She stared right at me, and licked her lips with that black tongue. I hollered like a banshee, barreling for the door. I dropped the flashlight and grabbed the door handle. I pulled and screamed, managing to get it open about an inch or so, but before I could reach my fingers through to pull harder, her arm went around my neck, choking me. I jerked and wiggled, still screaming–so panicked I could have died on the spot. She brought her right hand up and scratched my face with her nails. It stung like snake venom.

"I knew I had to do something quick. I grabbed at that small opening in the door and held on for dear life. She tried to tug me back, but I wouldn't let go. The door opened just enough for a scrawny kid like me to slip through. I kicked at her, still screaming. All that squirming did some good because for a split second she let go, and I shot out of there as fast as I could. And with the adrenaline pumping through me right then . . . that was the fastest I'd ever ran. I made it downstairs and nearly to the front door. Just as I got there, I could see her outline in the shadows, blocking my way. I shifted quickly and headed for the window. No time to stop and open it. I kicked the glass with my shoe, breaking it into jagged shards. I jumped through, cutting my arm as I leapt. I guess luck was on my side because the iron gate was open. I ran out of there and down the street, and I didn't stop until a police car came by and made me. I collapsed on the ground."

After a few moments of silence, Anne realized he'd finished the story. "They took you to jail, right?" she prompted.

He nodded, rubbing his closed eyes with his thumb and forefinger.

"What happened to your friends?" Juniper asked him. Her voice sounded foreign.

"I'm not sure you could call them friends," Mr. Nicholson said. "But one police officer went and asked them to validate my story. He said they were home in bed . . . didn't know what I was talking about. The police concluded the scratches on my face were from the broken window. They drove me home, and my father had to pay a fine for my misbehavior. He probably would have punished me good except I took to my bed and didn't move or speak for three solid days. It was another week before I could bring myself to talk about it. 'Course, no one believed me."

"I believe you," Anne said, shutting off the tape recorder. "I believe every word." Anne reached into her backpack and brought out the picture she'd taken of the attic window. "Mr. Nicholson, do you think this is her?"

He took the photo in his rickety hand and glanced down. Just as quickly he dropped it to the floor, his face pinched in pain. “I’m tired. I think I need to rest now.”

“Thank you,” Anne said, gathering her things. “Sorry if we upset you.”

He kept his head lowered on his hand, saying nothing.

As the Fortune Tellers Club left the bedroom, the toddler in the sagging diaper ran past them. “Poo Pa!”

CHAPTER 12

A Triple Dose of Divination

The girls rode away faster than before. The sky had clouded up again, and the threat of rain was in the air. No one spoke until they reached Anne's house.

Sitting in their usual circle, Gena began to play it up. "Phew! I'm glad I'm not sleeping alone at home tonight. Have you ever been so totally creeped out?"

"No," Juniper said. "But my nerves are so tight right now, one wrong move and I'll propel to the ceiling."

Anne said nothing. She hugged her knees, rocking back and forth, mentally computing everything Mr. Nicholson had said. The window was no longer broken, but then again, if someone thought enough of the place to put a historical marker in front, they'd probably fix the window too. Or maybe that's why Mr. Nicholson's father was ordered to pay a fine.

She reached in her backpack and removed the picture. The face glancing out through the haze looked like a normal enough face. No bulging eyes or black tongue. Could Mr. Nicholson have made all that up?

Gena and Juniper continued their silly babbling. "You know," Gena said. "I'm so freaked out that if I were a Saturday matinee movie, I'd be *Scream.*"

Juniper clicked her tongue. "You never saw *Scream.* It's rated R."

"I didn't see it at the theater, but I watched it on cable." She gave Juniper a "so there!" look.

Juniper let out a nervous giggle. "I'd be *The Bride of Frankenstein.* That story made my hair stand up."

Gena laughed and gave Juniper a nudge on the arm. "Hey, Mr. Nicholson would be *Psycho!*"

Anne turned briskly toward Gena. "That's mean! He was a nice man. He didn't *have* to talk to us."

"Well, right now," Gena said, "I'm wishing he hadn't. That was scarier than all the big, hairy insects in every bathroom in the world."

Anne sighed and went back to her rocking motion. Her mind stayed focused on Boogerman's house.

Gena stretched out on the floor, rubbing her eyes. "I guess this answers the question of whether or not to go inside the house."

"Yeah," Anne said. "We should definitely go in."

Gena shot back up into a sitting position. "What? That's insane!"

"More than ever, I've got to see for myself."

"Anne, get a grip," Gena said, her voice slow and calm. "Think back to right before we got here. A ghost story about a hideous lady with razor sharp nails? Ring a bell?"

"I've got to see for myself."

Gena groaned in frustration. "Am I the only one who just experienced *Nightmare on Elm Street?*"

"Good one," Juniper said, giving Gena a high five.

Anne looked Gena in the eyes. "Do you have a better suggestion?"

"Yes. Do your report on the Statue of Liberty."

Anne wheeled back, not wanting to hear it. She'd already come this far with her research, and she desperately felt the need to find out more. And going inside was the best way. "Do you think I'm nuts?" she asked Juniper.

"Yes, but that's beside the point. I think we should settle this the way we settle everything. Fortune telling." She reached into her overnight bag and pulled out her pendulum.

"Wouldn't it be better if we used cards?" Anne asked.

"Wait!" Gena rummaged through her overnight bag too. "Remember this?" She pulled out the cube-shaped eraser that she'd turned into her Mystic Genie.

"Hey!" Juniper said with a smile. "You still use that thing?"

"Only for emergencies." Gena rubbed it between her palms. "And right now, I consider this a matter of life or death."

Anne rolled her eyes, shaking her head. "Don't get all drama queen on us, Gena. I really need your help."

"That's up to the Mystic Genie," Gena replied, clutching it near her heart.

"I've got an idea," Juniper said. "Anne, get a regular deck of cards."

Anne hopped up and quickly retrieved them. Juniper's ideas usually were the best, and she was anxious to hear this one. "Got 'em," she said, settling back down in the circle.

Juniper pinched the string of her pendulum between her thumb and forefinger, letting the pendant hang loose. "We'll have a predict-off."

"Huh?" Gena said.

Juniper nodded once toward Gena. "Get ready to roll your Genie."

Gena jiggled it in her hand.

"Anne," Juniper continued, "shuffle the cards. Okay, should we go into the Shady Lane House, or not? On the count of three, we close our eyes and concentrate. When I say 'now,' open your eyes. That's when Gena rolls the Genie. And you turn up one card."

"Just one?" Anne asked.

"Yes or no. Red for yes. Black for no. Ready?"

"I'm ready to curl up in a little ball and forget about Boogerman's house," Gena said in a wimpy voice.

"You may get your wish," Anne said, secretly hoping for a yes answer, though.

Anne shuffled. Gena shook her Mystic Genie. Juniper sat perfectly still, pendulum extended.

"One . . . two . . . three."

Anne shut her eyes, and clumsily shuffled. *Say yes! Say yes! Say yes! Yes! Yes! Yes! Yes! Yes! Yes! Yes! Yes! Yes! Yes!*

"Now."

Anne opened her eyes and without another thought, turned up the first card. Red! Juniper's pendulum swung in a clockwise motion. Gena tossed the Mystic Genie. It rolled on top of the Queen of Hearts that Anne had laid down. Anne's heart did a high jump when she saw the answer. *Without a doubt!*

Gena fell backward on the floor, pounding her hands and shaking her head. "Nooooooo! Don't make me go inside that house."

"Why not?" Anne asked. "It looks like the good vibes are on our side."

"I say best two out of three," Gena whined.

"Technically, that was the best two out of three," Juniper explained. "If only *two* of the predictions had been the same, we'd have gone with it."

Gena curled up in a little ball. "I love you guys, but you really keep my life on the edge."

Anne smiled, knowing Gena was just overreacting. "If you don't want to go, you don't have to."

"Really?" Gena said, sitting up.

"Yeah, maybe you could go to the mall with Beth and Nicole instead."

Juniper giggled. Gena fell back to the floor. "I'd rather take my chances with an ape-wild ghost."

"It's settled then," Anne said, beaming throughout. "Tomorrow, we go inside."

CHAPTER 13

Breaking In

The overcast sky and strong winds brought Boogerman's house to life. Its gray wood seemed even darker still, like heavy smoke or oil. The trees and bushes rattled in the heavy gusts, and a broken shutter snapped an uneven drumbeat against it. *It's looking at us,* Anne thought.

The Fortune Tellers Club stood just outside the gate, holding tightly to their bikes. Anne had packed her recorder and camera. Juniper had brought a flashlight. Gena had lugged her old

Louisville Slugger, a baseball bat made for swinging hard.

Anne squinted against the damp wind, her hair whipping wildly across her face.

"Maybe we should come back another time," Gena said. "We're about to face the storm of the century."

Anne wasn't sure if Gena meant the weather or what they'd face inside, but she wasn't turning back now. *How appropriate. Haunted house. Storm. The only thing missing is a clock striking midnight.* "We won't get wet inside." She laid her bike flat, then opened the iron gate. Letting go quickly, the wind grabbed the gate and slammed it against the fence.

Juniper stood close, shoulder to shoulder with Anne, but once they got into the yard, Gena moved up, clinging to her arm. Anne could feel her trembling. But the jittering wasn't only Gena. Anne's nerves were also stretched as tight as rubber bands.

An eerie yowling floated with the wind, nearly sending Gena on top of her.

"What was that?" Juniper asked.

"Banshees!" Gena said. "Let's go home, pleeeeeease!"

Anne stopped and gripped Gena's arm. "Cats. There are wild cats in the rose garden around back."

The cats' cries sounded mournful and creepy. "Let's hurry," Anne said. They moved on.

Anne paused a moment when they reached the backyard. The roses looked darker too, like blood. And there were at least seven or eight wiry cats, pawing underneath the bushes. Their meows sounded woeful, like women crying.

As the three girls neared the small back porch, they automatically turned their heads upward toward the attic window. Other than an eternity of filth, the window looked like any other tiny window. No haze or smoke or ghosts peered out.

"We'll go through here," Anne told them, stepping up to the backdoor. She turned the doorknob.

"Did you really expect it to be open?" Juniper asked.

Anne shook her head. "No, but I always believe in trying the easy stuff first."

"Oh really?" Gena said. "Because this seems like the hardest social studies report I've ever heard of."

Anne ignored her and studied the back entrance. She looked at the pipes that outlined the back-door. They disappeared into the wall just above it. Over that was a rectangular window, about the size of her bed pillow. "I could crawl through there."

"Yeah . . . if you can figure out how to get up there," Juniper said.

Anne smiled. "Hold this."

She handed over the sling bag that held the camera and tape recorder, then she reached up, grabbed one of the pipes, and shimmied up. She pulled herself higher and higher, like a caterpillar inching up a wall. Her palms burned from the rough pipe, but she only had to go as high as the door. Reaching the bulky fitting where the pipe turned, she held on. One more giant tug brought her all the way to the top. She squeezed her knees against the pipe to hold herself still. A clap of thunder startled her, almost making her slip.

"How are you going to open it?" Juniper asked.

Good question. Anne looked at the window for a moment, her hands burning from hanging on. There was no latch anywhere on the outside of the window. She rested her arm on the top pipe that turned above the door. Reaching out, she pushed on the window. Nothing. Did she really expect it to open?

"This isn't working," Gena said. "Let's go now before we get hit by lightning."

Anne clung to the pipe. Reaching out again, she dug her nails into the side of the window, and pulled. "Ouch!" A splinter the size of a toothpick embedded itself in her fingernail. Using her teeth, she pulled it out. Several droplets of blood curled under her nail, turning it purple.

"Forget it," Juniper said. "You're not going to get it open."

Juniper was right. Anne sighed, her arms and legs trembling from clinging to the pipe. As Anne pushed herself back to the part of the pipe beside the door, a crash of thunder boomed louder than ever. It felt like an earthquake, shaking everything, and miraculously knocking the window open. "Whoa!" She looked down at Juniper and Gena. "I must have loosened it before."

Juniper smiled up. "Looks like the force is with us!"

Gena wasn't smiling. "Or maybe something in there pushed it out. Anyway, it's only open partway. You can't squeeze in through there."

Anne pulled herself up again and grabbed the edge of the window. It was held open by two thin, rusted chains. "Yes I can."

Thankful to have something bigger to hang onto, she curled herself above the window and prepared to slide in. With a muffled *pop!* one of the chains broke, tilting the window to the side, causing her to lose momentum. Anne clutched the window frame and turned herself around. Sliding in feet first, she let go, dropping to the ground as easily as doing a tumbling cheer at a football game.

"Ta da!" she said, opening the door for Juniper and Gena, who both looked like they had an advanced case of the willies.

The girls stepped in, looking around. The entire kitchen was covered in a blanket of dust. Cobwebs filled the sink, and hung from the light fixture.

"Did I forget to mention I have allergies?" Gena said, her voice squeaking.

"You do not." Juniper's voice echoed off the walls.

Gena held the baseball bat high over her head. "Shhh, something may come crashing down on us."

Anne looked at Gena. "If that were the case, it would have crashed down during that last jolt of thunder." She was happy for the suggestion to stay quiet, though. Creeping through the room, she felt a mixture of fear and jubilation. *I can't believe I'm finally inside!* But she was also anxious to get out of the moldy-smelling kitchen and into a more open part of the house.

As they wandered through the dining room, and into the den, the sky opened and a massive downpour hit the roof. The windows, already clouded with a film of dirt, looked even grayer with the sheets of rain coming down outside.

Gena sneezed.

"*Gesundheit,*" Anne said.

Gena wiped her nose on the hem of her tee shirt. "I hope that's a word to ward off evil spirits."

"Nope," Anne said. "My mother says it when I sneeze. It means health."

Gena rested the baseball bat on her shoulder. "Close enough."

Juniper stopped suddenly and looked at Anne. "Is it just me, or did the temperature suddenly drop about twenty degrees?"

"I'm chilly too," Anne replied. "It must be the storm."

"And all this time I thought it was panic shaking me out of my sneakers," Gena said.

They rounded the corner out of the den to find a wide, open staircase just on the other side of the wall.

"I'm not going up there," Gena said, her bat at the ready again.

Anne wasted no time going up. “Fine. Stay down here alone.”

Gena was practically on her heels, bumping into her with nearly every step.

As the staircase wound around, Anne half expected to see the Gray Lady standing at the top, waiting for them. But all that was waiting was a large hallway with an ornate bookcase against one wall. “Weird place to put a bookcase.”

“Weird house,” Juniper added.

Gena didn’t say a word. Anne noticed that her face was about as ashy as the dust, and wondered if it was really fair making her come with them. Gena was afraid of everything.

The hallway was lined with doors, most opening into large rooms that Anne figured were bedrooms at one time. A couple of them had fireplaces. She felt like Jonah inside the whale. The house seemed to swallow them.

“Okay,” Gena said, her voice an octave higher. “No ghosts or gray ladies or demons tolling bells. Take some pictures for your report and let’s go . . . please?”

"Not just yet," Juniper said, opening a small door at the end of the hall. They all peered in at the hidden stairs leading up. At the very top was a small rounded door.

"That's it," Anne said, reaching in and clicking on her tape recorder. "That's the attic."

CHAPTER 14

Trapped

"Noooooo!" Gena shouted, causing Anne to jump. "I don't think we should go in there."

Anne wished Gena had stayed home. "We don't have to go in," she said firmly. "But I've come this far. I'm at least going to peek inside."

"And what if she's in there? You know . . . hanging around with her black tongue and all."

Juniper took Gena's arm. "You can stay here. Anne and I will look inside."

"Oh no," Gena said. "You're not leaving me alone."

"Holy donuts, Gena!" Anne said. "We're not leaving you completely alone. We'll be right there—seven steps up. Gosh, we could've had a peek by now."

Gena nodded toward the steps and held the Louisville Slugger up again, poised to knock off any ghostly head that got in the way.

"Great," Juniper said. "You stand guard."

Anne took the steps slowly, Juniper so close she could hear her shaky breath. Anne felt like a ghost herself. Her body moved automatically, without thought or emotion. She thought her heart should be pounding, but just like her footsteps, it was silent and steady. But when she reached the small door, her mouth suddenly went as dry as a dog biscuit.

"Open it," Juniper whispered, crouching behind her.

Anne reached for the knob. For such a little door, it was difficult to open. She tugged, inching it open slowly. The way it scraped the floor gave her an odd chill. She didn't open it fully, just enough for her and Juniper to scope out the inside.

The two girls stood close together, peering in. "Ew," Juniper said. "This place is just nasty. Look at the dirt on the floor."

Anne was too busy looking at the beams in the middle of the ceiling. That piece of rope was still there, just as Mr. Nicholson had described it. Only it looked totally black now. "Do you think that's the actual rope?" Anne asked, snapping a picture with her camera.

"Uh-uh," Juniper said. "Probably a joke. Some kids broke in and tied it there, I bet."

"It looks like it's been there for an eternity." Anne's eyes skimmed the room, then focused on the window. "There it is. That's the window she was standing by."

"What do you guys see?" Gena said. "Is it scary?"

"Just an empty old attic," Juniper answered. "You should come see for yourself."

"Uh . . . that's okay. I'm good," Gena stuttered.

Anne pushed on the door to open it more. She stepped in.

Juniper grabbed her arm, tugging. "Hey, I thought we were just going to peek in, not take a tour."

"I just need a quick look at the window," Anne said, hoping those words would reassure her. "I'll only be a second."

As she crossed the room, she heard Gena calling up, "What's Anne doing?"

"Never mind," Juniper said. "She's just looking at something. It's no big deal."

Anne's nerves rippled as she got closer. She took a few pictures as she walked. A layer of dirt was everywhere, including the glass pane of the window. She ran her finger across it, pulling off cobwebs, but no dirt came off. That's when reality snapped. The glass was frosted with a gray tint. Sort of like stained glass, only all one color. *Any* person looking through here would appear gray.

Anne checked out the footprints on the floor, just under the window. They weren't all hers. Feeling squeamish, she headed back to Juniper. "Someone's been up here."

"Are you sure it was a real live person and not a ghost?" Juniper asked.

"I don't know," Anne said, looking back through the door. "But I don't think ghosts leave footprints, do they?"

She saw Gena sigh as they came down, obviously relieved to see them. "Can we leave now?" she asked.

"I guess so," Anne answered. She tried to keep the disappointment out of her voice. She was happy to have the pictures of Boogerman's house, but she somehow thought there'd be more. She really had wanted to meet up with the Gray Lady, even if it did scare the life out of her. This could have been the report of a lifetime. They walked down the hall, and Anne felt as deflated as Gena had looked when Anne had appeared from the attic.

As they headed back to the winding staircase, Anne bumped against the bookcase set against the wall. *Why would anyone put a bookcase in such a stupid place?*

Gena ran down the stairs, obviously anxious to be as far away from Boogerman's house as possible. "Wait up!" Juniper called, running after her.

Anne slowly descended, taking each step one at a time. There had to be more. She felt it as surely as she felt the unnatural chill in the air. She stopped and glanced back up. Something wasn't right. *The bookcase.* Her bump had obviously moved it some. Not much, but enough that she could see a door jamb at the very top, just behind it.

She started to call out to the other Fortune Tellers Club members, but figured they were already out the door, waiting on their bikes. She hurried back to the bookcase. It had moved. Just an inch. Reaching her fingers in behind it, she slid them down until they stopped against a cold metal object. Anne tinkered with the metal, realizing it was a latch. Flipping it open, she pulled on the bookcase. To her amazement, it opened out quite easily. Behind it was a door.

Why did they have to rush off? Anne thought, turning the antique crystal knob on the hidden door. She opened it inward–into the darkness inside. *Darn!* Juniper had the flashlight. Anne thought she should go and get it from her, but soon her eyes adjusted enough to make out the outlines of the room. Furniture. Chairs. Small tables. A fancy writing desk. Anne stepped farther into the room. The door closed behind her, leaving her in a black void of nothingness. She couldn't see her hand in front of her face. Feeling her way through the darkness, she found the door again and twisted the knob. It wouldn't open. She jerked and pulled it. Nothing.

I won't panic. I won't panic. I won't panic . . .

"HELP!"

She was trapped.

CHAPTER 15

The Diary

"Please! Juniper! Gena! Where are you?" Anne pounded on the door until her fists burned. *Where were they?* Surely they'd come back looking for her. Fear got the better of her, but she swallowed it back. She stopped to think things through. *Focus, Anne—focus.*

She felt her way back through the blinding darkness, bumping against a chair. The writing desk . . . that's where she wanted to be. Maybe there was something in the drawer that she could use to pry the door open with. She wandered about in what she hoped was the general direction of it. With her hands feeling the air before her, she took careful sliding steps. Finally . . . she touched it. *Bingo!* Anne let out her clutched breath.

The drawer opened with only a bit of waggling. She dipped her hands in, rummaging through the various items, the largest being a book. "Ouch!" Her ring finger stung like a wasp had attacked. She drew it up to her mouth, tasting the metal tang of blood. *Just what I need right now. A paper cut.*

Shutting the drawer, Anne carefully patted the top of the desk for something . . . anything useful. She found it. Yes! A shape that could only be a large candle. With her left hand gripping it, she used her right to feel around for matches. *Yeah!* The gods were on her side. A tin canister of matches sat next to it. *Let there be light.*

The container was nothing like a regular match box or those small book of matches that Anne had seen all her life. Where do you strike these matches? The desk top was far too smooth, but there was no polish underneath. The wood was unfinished and rough. Anne quickly grabbed a match and tried it. She might as well have tried striking a toothpick. Nothing happened. Not even a spark. *Please!* she thought, trying not to panic. She tried harder, accidentally breaking the match in half.

"Aaargh!" Grabbing another, she flicked it across the bottom of the desk. "Come on." It didn't light either. *Maybe they're too old to work anymore.* She tried striking it three times before giving up and grabbing another.

"This is not happening." Her panic echoed around the room. "Light! Light!"

Only three matches remained in the canister. *Work this time . . . please.* She took one of them out, and with a shaky hand, zapped it across the bottom of the desk. With a swoosh the room lit up for a moment.

"Yes!" Her breath made the flame quiver. *Don't celebrate yet,* she thought, thankful that her excitement didn't blow out the match. She could see the outline of the candle now, and it lit right away, filling the room with a brassy glow. Huge shadows, like giant monsters, loomed over her.

Anne wanted to pick up the candle and carry it back to the door, but she was too afraid it would go out. She couldn't take the blinding darkness again. Instead she sat down, looking around the room at the dusty antique furniture. The chairs were carved with fancy swirls, and the upholstery looked like it had once been a gold satin—even the one she sat in. One chair had a small, round table beside it covered with a dingy, lace doily and an oil lamp. Everything looked ancient. But the most intriguing feature in the room was the Spinet piano that stood hidden in the darkness of the corner. The sight of it sent prickles through Anne's flesh. Was this the source of the ghostly music?

Can people really die of fright? she wondered, turning back to the drawer again for a better look. Surely there was a letter opener or something she could use to jimmy the door. The book she had felt earlier lay in the middle. Anne pulled it out and read the cover. *Diary.* She opened it and fanned the pages. Nearly every page was filled with faded handwriting, most illegible. Turning back to the front page, she could just make out the name written there–Isabelle Davis.

"Anne!" The voice was distant, but definitely Juniper's.

"I'm trapped in here! Help!" Anne ran to the door.

"Where?"

"Behind the bookcase by the stairs!"

"How'd you get back there?" That voice was Gena's.

"Come on, you guys, get me out!"

She heard pushing and scratching just on the other side of the wall. "Are you moving it?"

"We can't," Juniper said. "It won't budge."

"Of course it will," Anne called through the wall. "I moved it. There's a latch that opens it. Peek behind the bookcase and you'll see it."

She heard muffled, prodding sounds. "Are you sure? We can't find it."

Anne took a deep breath to steady herself. "I'm sure. That's how I got in here. Come on, look! It's there. I know it is."

"So, it's just like in those scary movies when someone pulls out a book and the bookcase opens?" Gena said.

"No. There are no books on that bookcase. It's a latch . . . behind it. You've got to *feel* it. It's right there!"

"Anne," Juniper said, sounding more serious than ever. "How did it latch itself back? How did you get trapped?"

Anne stood, hearing her own heart pumping wildly. How *did* she get locked in? The only way would be by someone on the outside who wanted to trap her. "I don't know for sure how it happened, but it did. Please get me out . . . now!"

"We'll have to go for help," Juniper said. "Do you want Gena to stay behind and talk to you while I go?"

"Forget it," Gena whimpered. "I'll go and you stay."

"Whatever!" Anne called, ready to claw her way through. "Just hurry. I'm really, really scared."

Anne heard footsteps running down the stairs. Then silence. "Juniper? A-a-are you still there?"

"Yeah . . . creeped out, but still here."

"That makes two of us," Anne said, wanting more than anything to be away from the cobwebs and the shadows.

"Listen," Juniper said. "I'm going to look for something around here to pry open the bookcase."

"No, don't leave me!"

"I won't go out of the house, I promise."

"Juniper!" Anne felt the panic drumming in her throat.

"Let's be realistic," Juniper said, her voice shaky. "The quicker I find some way to get you out, the faster we can get the heck out of here."

"I don't like this," Anne answered, slumping down and hugging her knees.

"I'll just be a minute," Juniper said. "Stay put."

"Stay put? That's not funny."

"Sorry. Just count to a hundred or something," Juniper suggested. "Keep your mind busy. I won't be far."

Anne hugged her knees tighter, tears stinging her cheeks. *Juniper won't be far,* she told herself. *Keep your mind busy. Keep your mind busy . . .*

She repeated this mantra as she trudged back to the desk, tears streaming down her cheeks. She wiped them on the back of her hand and sniffled. Maybe reading an entry or two in the diary would keep her mind off the goblins and shadows that played in her head. Leaning forward, she turned the page. The first entry was dated September 28, 1904. Anne squinted to read the words.

> *They came to see me again. All those children. They looked so prim and polite in their pinafores and smart bowties. I thought they'd be grown by now, but they looked just the*

> *same. Each sat at the piano and played the concerto we worked so hard on perfecting. Then, one by one, they gave me an eager kiss and thanked me for all those years of lessons. So sweet. Every one of them. I didn't mind them coming by, but I wish they hadn't brought the others. The children I never had. It pained me to see them, looking at me with big round eyes. "It's not my fault," I told them. I think they forgave me before they faded away. I hate it when things appear and fade like that. It makes my head ache terribly.*

Anne scooted the chair back, rubbing the chills on her arms. *Freaky. Mrs. Davis had obviously gone nuts. Why else would children fade in and out? Especially ones who'd never been born.* She reached over again and flipped to the middle of the diary.

> *April 2, 1905*
> *Today is my wedding anniversary. I wish Carlton were here to help me celebrate. Anniversaries are more fun when both the husband*

> *and wife are together. I baked a cake with lemon frosting and cut a slice with piano wire. That would have been Carlton's piece. I didn't eat any. Instead, I scraped it all onto the roses for the cats to eat. They look so thin. They didn't eat it either. The rain will wash it away. I put the piano wire back under my handkerchiefs in the bureau.*

Anne's hand trembled as she flipped another page. Before she got a chance to read it, a noise filtered through the door. The bookcase unlatched, and the hidden door opened.

"Juniper!" Anne called, relieved. But when she whipped around in her chair, it wasn't Juniper she saw. A haggard woman in a gray tunic approached her. Her wild, gray hair hung about her shoulders, her face was the color of stone. Anne gripped the chair to keep from fainting.

CHAPTER 16

Written Confessions

The woman in gray moved a step or two closer. "What have you got there?"

Anne wasn't sure what she meant. Her fear still shook her, causing her to feel lightheaded. She was conscious of the fact that her body swooned with dizziness.

"Are you okay?" the woman asked, coming even closer. "You look as though you've seen a ghost."

"You're the Gray Lady," Anne whispered.

The woman looked down at her clothes. "I guess I am. Who are you?"

Anne took a breath and held it. She steadied herself. "Anne," she said. Confusion overcame her wooziness. Although her knees still felt like water, she couldn't help but wonder. *This is the ghost that chased Mr. Nicholson out the window?*

"You've found something," the woman said.

Anne stepped back, touching the diary.

"Looks interesting," the woman said, stepping toward her at a slow pace.

"It's a diary." Anne watched the woman approach. Her face was lined with wrinkles, but her smile seemed soft and tender. She looked more like someone's sweet old granny than a vicious apparition. "Who are you?"

The woman hesitated. "Liz Browning."

"Well, thank you for rescuing me, Miss Browning. We should leave before the door closes and traps us." Anne waited for the woman to turn, but she continued standing near Anne, peering around her.

“May I?” the old woman asked, her interest obviously on the diary, not Anne. She lay a withered finger on the page and read. “The ranting of a mad woman, wouldn’t you say?”

“No,” Anne said. Suddenly she felt protective of the diary. It was her find, and she wasn’t going to turn it over to some woman who appeared out of nowhere. *Nowhere?* “What are you doing here, Miss Browning?”

“I could ask the same of you, dear.”

Anne shuffled back a bit. “I’m researching. For a school report.”

The woman nodded. “This house frightens you, doesn’t it?”

“This house frightens everyone,” Anne stated.

The woman lowered her chin, looking worn and weary. Anne wondered if she should offer her the chair. When the woman raised her head again, her eyes looked deep and dark as canyons. “It has always frightened me too.”

Anne watched the woman’s wandering gaze. She seemed genuinely intrigued by the room. But Anne was still on her guard. Where did this woman come from? And how did she know about the bookcase? "So why are you here?"

The woman moved past Anne, walking around and sitting gently on the chair. "You could say I'm here for my own liberation."

"Liberation?" *Get to the point,* Anne thought.

"I've been hiding out here," the woman said. "Doing my own research. I want to know what really happened to that woman. The one who lived here long, long ago."

Anne pulled the diary closer. "I think I've stumbled onto the answer to that. I just don't understand how that can liberate you though. How do you know about this house? And this room?"

"I've been hiding out. Trying to undo my fears. So many. So, so many."

Anne was losing patience. "No disrespect, Miss Browning, but how is hiding out in a haunted house going to undo your fears? I would think they'd add a ton more."

"Do you know who I am?" the woman asked.

Anne didn't, but obviously this lady was some celebrity or something. *A famous actress?* Anne decided she didn't look very "Hollywood." "Are you an author?"

The woman's gaze settled on her hands, folded and trembling. "Ah . . . a writer, a poet, a bard."

"I knew it!" Anne said. "And you were looking at me the other day while I was taking pictures. I caught you in one of my photos, looking out the window."

The woman hinted at a smile.

"The glow!" Anne shouted, causing the woman to flinch. "A laptop. You must have been writing by the window. That bluish-silver glow was from your computer."

"I love to write," the woman said. "It calms me." She pulled the diary toward her, and turned the pages. "I think you might find some interesting information here for your school assignment."

Anne watched as Miss Browning turned to the last entry.

"Oh dear. This seems to be the end of it." The woman stood, ushering Anne to sit. Anne took that as a suggestion to read. She looked down at the page.

"What does it say?" the woman asked.

Anne read aloud.

July 26, 1904

I can no longer allow this. Living, yet not living. Not even existing. Carlton comes to haunt me. My dreams are filled with him, and the heinous crime I committed upon him. I, a civil woman. How could I? Is it possible for this frail body to possess so much emotion? Strength? Rage? Passion ruled me. Passion, as strong as the piano wire I used to strangle him.

And yet I am weak. Only the weak would take the life of a loved one, rather than see him living his life in the arms of another woman. And Kate. I live with her blood on my hands and soul as well.

But what of passion? Why so vile a rage? Others channel their passion in creative ways. I could have written poetry. A sonnet of my woe. Or a cantata. Expressed my anger through music.

And so I cannot face another day. Another hour. Another minute.

Oh, how I long to be buried in the rose garden, next to the grave I prepared for Carlton. Yet, I will leave no such instructions behind. I am not worthy of a legacy.

So ends the diary of Isabelle Davis
—Wife and Teacher

Anne's voice had gone to a whisper. A new fear crept in. "Omigosh!" She looked at Miss Browning, whose eyes glistened with tears.

"Miss Browning, do you know what this means?"

The woman nodded, rubbing her hands.

"Mrs. Davis murdered her husband! She buried him in the rose garden."

The woman stood, facing Anne. "Take the diary, my dear. You now have much, much more for your assignment."

Anne smiled, although she was still overwhelmed by what she'd just read. "Thank you,

Miss Browning. Now I really should go. Are you coming?"

"Yes." They walked to the doorway, stepping through. Anne closed the door and the bookcase. She clutched the diary close.

"Go ahead," the woman said. "Go find your friend."

"My friend?" Miss Browning had seen Juniper?

"Yes. Don't worry about me. I've got everything I need now."

Anne scurried down the stairs, then turned back. "I'll look out for your latest novel. I bet you'll have lots to put in it."

The woman gave her a slight wave.

Anne rushed down the stairs and looked around for Juniper. No sign of her inside. She ran out the backdoor, careful not to look toward the rose garden. Knowing a body was buried there was enough to keep her moving–fast! She ran around the yard, bumping into Juniper coming from the other direction.

"You got out?" Juniper said, flashing a huge crowbar.

"You were supposed to stay with me–in the house. Where's Gena?"

"She's not back yet, but look what I found out in the shed. I was going to bust you out." Juniper held the crowbar up for Anne to see.

"Yeah, well, look what I found," Anne said.

Juniper lowered the crowbar and raised an eyebrow. "What's that?"

Anne held the diary to her chest. "My A+."

CHAPTER 17

Grounded

For the next few days, Anne felt like a queen—especially while taping the newspaper article into her scrapbook. She ran a finger over the headlines.

One-Hundred-Year-Old Mystery Solved!

It showed Anne smiling proudly at the camera, diary in hand. There were two pictures of Boogerman's house, one from the late 1800s, and another from last Sunday afternoon. There were also some gruesome pictures of the police digging up the wild roses in back.

The attention at school was overwhelming. But her glory came with a price. For the first time in her life, she was grounded. Mostly for disobeying a no trespassing sign and putting herself and her friends in danger. No phone. No friends. No television. No Internet (except for school research).

A knocking at her bedroom window late Tuesday afternoon sent her jolting off her bed. "What are you doing here? Are you trying to get me grounded for life?"

Juniper and Anne looked in through the window. Juniper waved a newspaper up and down. "You've got to see this!"

Anne raised the window. "Lucky for you my parents aren't home right now."

Anne stopped when she saw the photo. It did look like the lady in the window, but Anne's shock hit a different note inside. "This isn't Isabelle Davis, the Gray Lady. This is Liz Browning."

Gena turned the paper around and looked down at the picture. "The writer lady?"

"Yes, I'm positive. I mostly saw her by candlelight, but I'm sure it's her."

"But look how old the photo is," Juniper said. "It has to be Isabelle Davis. Did you look that author up on the Internet? I'm still kinda fuzzy on what she was doing there, anyway."

Anne raced to the computer and pulled up the search engine. She typed quickly. Liz Browning. The results were not at all what she expected.

> Elizabeth Barrett Browning—Author, Poet, Bard. Elizabeth Barrett Browning, born March 6, 1806, was the fourth of twelve children. Though she lived a full life with an amazing body of published works, she is most known for her romantic poem, "How Do I Love Thee? Let me Count The Ways."

Flabbergasted, Anne looked at the newspaper photo again. "This can't be right."

Juniper stepped forward, getting closer to the screen. "Anne, this Elizabeth Barrett Browning is even popular these days, and she'd be around two hundred years old. That can't be who you met."

"I'm starting to feel weirded out again, you guys," Gena said.

Weirded out couldn't describe it. Anne sat down, looking over the newspaper article. Her eyes scanned the page until they fell on a particular diary passage from the Gray Lady.

> *And so I have naught but my piano and my poems to soothe me. They drive away the demons whose bells toll nightly in my dreams. As I remember my beloved Carlton, I again think of the poet, Elizabeth Barrett Browning, and how her words resonate my feelings.*
>
> *With my lost saints,*
> *—I love thee with the breath,*
> *Smiles, tears, of all my life!*
> *—and, if God choose,*
> *I shall but love thee better after death.*

Anne pointed to the paragraph, her throat too dry to swallow, much less speak.

"Anne, don't you see what this means?" Juniper said, her voice rising with excitement.

Anne nodded. "I spent time trapped in that room with the Gray Lady . . . a . . . a ghost."

"I wonder why she didn't attack you like she did Mr. Nicholson?" Gena asked.

Anne had no idea. She wondered about a lot of things. Did the Gray Lady lie to her so she wouldn't be scared? Did she want Anne to find the room and the diary? Was she tired of living (living?) with the guilt of what she'd done?

A car pulled into the driveway. "They're back already?" Juniper said. She and Gena practically fell over each other to get back out the window. "We'll talk about it tomorrow at school," Juniper said.

Anne closed the window and went back to the desk, looking at the newspaper photo. She took out the picture she'd taken of the back of Boogerman's house with the Gray Lady peering out the window. Although she was banned from the computer, she couldn't help sending one sneaky email.

To: Shutterbug Fallon
Subject: A New Hobby

Mr. Fallon, you may have seen me in the papers recently. Remember your offer to show me some pointers? Well, I'm sort of tied up right now, but maybe next week my mom could bring me by. I think I've developed a new style of photography that you can help me with. I really believe I have a hidden talent for capturing ghosts . . . or maybe it's really setting them free.

Anne Donovan

ABOUT DOTTI ENDERLE

Dotti Enderle is a Capricorn with E.S.P.—extra silly personality. She sleeps with the Three of Cups tarot card under her pillow to help her dream up new ideas for the Fortune Tellers Club. Dotti lives in Texas with her husband, two daughters, a cat, and a pesky ghost named Shakespeare. Learn more about Dotti and her books at:

www.fortunetellersclub.com